Helen Chapman

RISING STARS

NASEN House, 4/5 Amber Business Village, Amber Close, Amington, Tamworth, Staffordshire, B77 4RP

Rising Stars UK Ltd.
7 Hatchers Mews, Bermondsey Street, London SE1 3GS
www.risingstars-uk.com

Published 2011

Cover design: Burville-Riley Partnership
Illustrations: Bill Greenhead for Illustration Ltd. / iStock
Text design and typesetting: Geoff Rayner
Publisher: Gill Budgell
Publishing manager: Sasha Morton
Editorial consultants: Lorraine Petersen and Dee Reid
Editorial: Jane Wood

British Library Cataloguing in Publication Data.
A CIP record for this book is available from the British Library.

ISBN: 978-1-84680-977-4

Printed in the UK by Ashford Colour Press Ltd, Gosport, Hampshire

CONTENTS

MEET THE GANG-STARS!

Jacky

Tom

Natalie

Zeke

Aaron

?

Callum

Becca

Claire

Name:
Claire

Special skill:
Classical ballet

Good at:
Being graceful; working hard; spreading sunshine and happiness

Not so good at:
Understanding modern dance

Other info:
A real girlie girl who wears a lot of pink and loves the elegance of classical ballet.

PROFILES

Name:
Aaron

Special skill:
Martial arts; dancing
in a martial arts style

Good at:
Making excuses; being second-best

Not so good at:
Being the very best at anything that they
teach at ASH.

Other info:
More of a martial artist than a
performing artist. He and his cousin
Callum are really close – but maybe not
for ever ...

ABOUT ALL

STAR HIGH

Do you want to be a star?
Then ALL STAR HIGH SCHOOL
is the place for YOU.
We will make you
a star.

**Musicians,
dancers,
actors:
come see us now!**

Don't miss out!

CHAPTER

'Whooo-yaaahhh' yelled Aaron Farmer.
He had one eye shut and was holding
both hands up. He was ready to do a
double **karate** chop. If he had been
in a sports class nobody would have

minded, but he wasn't. He was at morning assembly!

At morning assembly students got the chance to be on stage and sing the school song. Aaron came up with a great idea to make this more interesting. He would sing but he would also do some **martial arts** moves. Aaron was dressed like a **ninja**. He wore a ninja hood and mask, drawstring trousers and jacket. Aaron thought he looked great. The students thought he looked great too. Principal Blake thought Aaron looked ridiculous and sent him off stage after only one 'whooo-yaaahhh'.

Aaron was into martial arts in a big way and knew he could defend himself if someone attacked him. To Aaron's surprise, All Star High's drama and singing teachers did not share his interest in martial arts.

Claire Stevens was into ballet in a big way. She wanted to become a famous ballerina. Claire took her ballet classes very seriously. When she got to dance class and saw Aaron there, still wearing his ninja outfit, she sighed. What a loser!

Aaron and Claire's dance class was going to be different today because they were getting a new dance teacher.

Aaron practised his martial arts moves in front of the wall of mirrors. He knew he would have to stop practising when the teacher got there. Aaron sighed. It felt like he was the only one at All Star High who liked the things he did.

Claire stood in front of the mirrors too and checked that she looked just how a ballerina should look. Her hair was in a neat bun and her pink tights had no holes. She put one hand on the handrail and did some warm-up exercises. Claire thought about the new teacher. 'I hope we get a famous ballerina,' she thought. 'That would be perfect.'

The door opened and their new teacher came into the room. He was definitely not a famous ballerina! He wore black tracksuit trousers, a tight red T-shirt and trainers.

'Haw-ar-ya?' he said. His voice sounded as if it came out of his nose.

The students all looked at each other. They had no idea what he'd just said. It must be his name.

'Good afternoon, Mr Hawarya,' they politely replied.

The new ballet teacher burst out laughing. 'I asked "how are you?"' he explained.

Nobody knew what to say. No

teacher had ever asked them how they were.

Claire finally spoke up. 'We're fine, thank you,' she said.

The teacher took out a photo from his bag. It was the school photo of the dance class students, with all their names on. He looked down at the photo to find out Claire's name. 'Thank you, Claire,' he said. 'I'm Mr Jay from New York City in the USA. And I want to see you guys DANCE!'

He went over to the music system and put in a CD. It was wild bongo music. The students just stared at Mr Jay.

'What do you want us to do?' Claire asked.

'Anything you like,' said Mr Jay. 'I just want to see you guys move.'

The class shuffled their feet and looked at each other. They were used to being told how to dance but one by one they started to move. They did jumps, leaps, flips, spins and every dance move that they ever wanted to do.

Now that Mr Jay had given him a free choice, Aaron took the chance to do some wild dance steps, using his martial arts moves. He did a big leap that nobody had ever seen him do before. In the middle of the leap, he kicked his legs like a kickboxer, then went into some ninja **poses** when he landed.

Claire was shocked. Aaron shouldn't be messing about in front of their new teacher. What would Mr Jay think of them? Claire knew Aaron well because they were members of the same gang. The Gang-Stars always helped each other. They had first met at an under-12s Music Club. It was so great to meet up again at high school that they started a gang.

Being in a gang didn't mean you had to put up with everything its members did. And Aaron was messing about.

It wasn't fair on her and the other students. What was Mr Jay going to think?

Claire knew she had to put things right. She danced right up to Aaron and hissed 'What are you doing? Mr Jay will think we're all hopeless if you keep messing about like that.'

Aaron looked at the other dancers. 'No, he won't,' he said. 'Everyone is doing their favourite dance steps. That's all that I'm doing, too.'

Claire didn't know what to say! Kickboxing was not a dance step. Aaron really was a loser.

Mr Jay watched every dancer. They

all had their own style and they were all very good. After a few more minutes he asked everyone to stop dancing.

Aaron was disappointed. 'I was enjoying that. I like mixing martial arts with dancing,' he said to Claire.

'I can see that,' said Claire. 'But they're two different skills, and they just don't go together.'

'Let me tell you what we've been doing,' said Mr Jay. 'That was a surprise audition. This class is going to do a dance performance of *Romeo and Juliet* and I had to decide which parts you are all going to get. Claire, you'll dance the role of Juliet.'

Claire could not believe her luck. Getting to dance the role of Juliet was so exciting. She was already thinking about what she would wear to the first rehearsal. Maybe something soft and floaty? She was so busy thinking about what to wear that she didn't hear Mr Jay when he said:

'Aaron, you'll dance the role of Romeo.'

Mr Jay went on telling the others what roles they would dance.

Aaron tapped Claire on her arm. 'Hey, I get to dance the role of Romeo,' he said. 'How great is that? You and me have both got the lead roles.'

Claire's mouth dropped open. She couldn't believe Mr Jay had given the part of Romeo to Aaron, after the way he had been messing about with his martial arts moves. She didn't know what to say.

'You guys can bail,' said Mr Jay.

The class stood there. Yet again they had no idea what he was talking about. '*Bail* means leave, go, depart,' he explained. He waved his arms. 'I'll put rehearsal times up on the noticeboard. Now shoo!'

CHAPTER

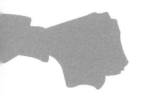

The first rehearsal was after school
the next day. Claire was excited about
being Juliet. She wore her best white
leotard and a long white skirt. She
hurried into the dance studio where

Mr Jay was waiting.

'We all know *Romeo and Juliet* is
a story about two teenagers in love,'
said Mr Jay. 'Their families are always
fighting and they aren't allowed to get
together. They get married secretly but
then everything goes wrong and it has
a very sad ending. No surprises there.'

He stopped talking for a moment
and looked at the students.

'But what I'm going to say next
might be a surprise,' He said. 'We
are going to do *Romeo and Juliet* as
a modern ballet. It's set on another
planet and you are going to be **aliens**.
Your families are still fighting so the

story is just the same.'

Aaron started to get more interested. Aliens sounded fun! A lot more fun than a soppy love story!

'Aliens!' said Claire. She looked at herself in the mirror. She knew she wouldn't be wearing a beautiful dress after all.

'I want to see you dance as if you are aliens,' said Mr Jay. 'Use your imagination and give me something new.'

Now Aaron started to get worried. He wasn't sure what to do. He had enjoyed mixing his martial arts moves with dance, but could he keep on doing that? Mr Jay wanted to see even more new things, and Aaron was running out of ideas.

Claire had made up her mind. Her alien would dance like a ballerina anyway. She danced across the floor using her favourite ballet steps. When she stopped she waited for Mr Jay to say how good she was.

'That's not what I want to see, Claire,' said Mr Jay. 'I want something new and exciting. Remember, you're meant to be on another planet. Try and move like an alien.'

Claire didn't like new and exciting, she was good at ballet, not modern dance. This time she danced like an alien who liked ballet!

Mr Jay still didn't like what she had done. 'Claire, watch Aaron's dance steps,' he said.

Claire watched Aaron do his silly martial arts jumps and hand chops.

'I want you to dance more like Aaron,' said Mr Jay. 'If you can't, I may have to give the part of Juliet to another dancer. Aaron, I want you to work out some more new moves and show Claire how to do them.'

Claire couldn't believe what Mr Jay had said. She was a much better dancer than Aaron, but now she had to copy the silly moves that he was doing. It was so unfair.

Mr Jay left the room and Claire went over to Aaron.

'Did you hear that?' she asked.

'I know you're cross at Mr Jay,' said Aaron. 'But don't take it out on me.'

But Claire did take it out on Aaron. When Aaron tried to show her how to do his martial arts moves, Claire wouldn't learn them. She didn't want to fight with Aaron but she couldn't help it. Martial arts moves had nothing to do with ballet.

'You're so selfish,' he said. 'Did you stop and think about me?'

'Why should I?' said Claire. 'Mr Jay thinks you're great.'

'I don't feel great,' said Aaron. 'I'm finding this really hard too. It was fun mixing dance with martial arts but now Mr Jay wants some more new moves and I've run out of ideas. I'm the lead male dancer, so I need lots of steps. I'll lose my part too, if I can't come up with some more ideas.'

'It seems like we're both stuck, then,' said Claire.

Claire knew she had to make up her mind. Would she do what Mr Jay wanted, and try something new, or should she just quit?

Claire really wanted to dance on stage. That was why she did ballet. Did it really matter if it wasn't normal ballet? Besides, Aaron needed her help with finding new steps. There were other types of modern dance steps she could try. The Gang-Stars didn't let each other down. Ever. Claire didn't want to fight with Aaron any more. She knew what she had to do. She looked at Aaron.

'I think I've got an idea,' she said. 'What are you doing tonight?'

CHAPTER

The Circus Acrobats show was in town
and Claire had a pair of tickets to the
show. She asked Aaron to go along to
the show with her.

'The acrobats are doing free circus

skills workshops this weekend,' she said. 'We can try to get some ideas from the show, and then learn how to do them at the workshops.'

Aaron couldn't wait to see the Circus Acrobats flying through the air on a **trapeze**. Claire was excited about seeing the show too. This time they were going to be watching the performers in a different way. This circus visit was a chance to get ideas for some new dance steps they could do together.

The show was wonderful. Claire liked the balancing acts. Some performers climbed up on each other's shoulders and stood up, and the acrobats were amazing to watch.

During the show a boy with spiky red hair turned around in his seat and said, 'Mr Jay is in the audience. Look.' He pointed across to the other side of the circus tent. Then the boy faced the front again.

'Who was that?' asked Claire.

'I don't know,' said Aaron. He looked over to where the boy had pointed. 'But he's right. There's Mr Jay and he's clapping loudly.'

After the show they went over to see Mr Jay.

'Hey, you two,' said Mr Jay. 'I didn't

know you were dating.'

'Oh no, we're not dating,' said Aaron, quickly.

Claire went red and shook her head. 'Oh no, that's not why we're here. We'd like to use some acrobatics for our *Romeo and Juliet* dance,' said Claire. 'We can learn some new moves at the circus skills workshops.' She crossed her fingers. What if Mr Jay said no?

'I want to do some trapeze moves too,' said Aaron. 'Would that be all right?'

Mr Jay seemed really pleased with their ideas. 'That sounds amazing!' he said. 'Go for it! I look forward to seeing what you come up with.'

Claire let out a big sigh of relief. They had lots of work to do, but now at least she and Aaron would be working as a team.

CHAPTER

Working as a team turned out to be
a lot of fun. Aaron and Claire had
a great time learning circus skills at
the workshops. At the end of the last
workshop, Mr Jay and the other Gang-

Stars came to see Aaron and Claire practising their new **routine** in the circus tent. Aaron started with a fight **sequence** using martial arts moves in an acrobatic dance style. It was amazing. He leapt up high, then he seemed to freeze in mid-air in a ninja pose.

'How is he doing that?' gasped Tom.

'With fantastic staging,' said Becca. 'Look, he's hanging from a trapeze wire. It's almost invisible.'

Slowly, Aaron turned his head to look at Claire, who was on a small platform high above the ground. She was spinning **en pointe**.

Aaron seemed to fly up to a trapeze bar, and soon he was swinging to and fro, doing amazing acrobatic moves. Claire kept spinning, then let herself fall, and Aaron caught her in his arms. They twirled together with an amazing mix of dance, acrobatics and martial arts moves. Their feet never touched the ground.

Mr Jay was very impressed. 'These new moves are working really well,' he said. 'But don't forget Romeo has to do more than just sweep Juliet off her feet.'

'Oh, yeah. That's right,' said Aaron. 'He has to kiss her.' He smiled at Claire.

Claire was surprised that Aaron knew that much about the story. She was even more surprised to find that she quite liked the idea of Aaron having to kiss her. Working as a team had brought them really close together.

'But in the alien *Romeo and Juliet* he will probably just ...' Aaron began.

'Just what?' asked Claire.

'Romeo will just, you know, slime her,' said Aaron.

Aaron picked up a plastic cup from the stage floor. It was one of the clown's props. He tipped it over Claire and poured out confetti, all over her head.

'You call that slimed?' said Claire.

'*This* is slimed.'

She grabbed the clown's squirt gun. She aimed and squirted gloop all over Aaron. He ran after her, and they got into a pretend fight, doing acrobatic leaps and flips to escape from each other. The Gang-Stars watched in surprise as Aaron and Claire chased, danced, leaped and laughed their way around the stage together.

'Well, I didn't see that coming,' said Natalie. 'I think we've got a real-life Romeo and Juliet here. It may not be a happy ending in *that* story, but something tells me it's going to be a different story for these two!'

GLOSSARY

acrobats – circus performers who can do tricks with their bodies

aliens – creatures from another planet

en pointe – French words, meaning ballet dancing on the tips of the toes

hand chops – making chopping moves with the hands in karate

karate – an Asian sport of self-defence, using hands and feet

leotard – a tight-fitting dance costume which looks similar to a swimming costume

martial arts – sports based on Asian combat skills

ninja – a mysterious traditional character linked with martial arts

pose – holding your body in a particular a position

routine – a set dance performance

sequence – a group of moves during a performance

trapeze – a high swing used for acrobatic shows

QUIZ

1   What is Aaron into in a big way?

2   What is Claire into in a big way?

3   What is the new teacher called?

4   Where is the new teacher from?

5   Why is Clare mad at Aaron in the dance class?

6   Which parts do Aaron and Claire get in the dance performance?

7   Why does Aaron need help?

8   Which show do Aaron and Claire go to see?

9   Where do Aaron and Claire learn their new acrobatic moves?

10 How does Claire slime Aaron?

ANSWERS

1 Martial arts

2 Ballet

3 Mr Jay

4 New York City, USA

5 Because she thinks he is messing about in front of their new teacher.

6 Romeo and Juliet

7 Because he is running out of ideas for new moves.

8 From the Circus Acrobats.

9 At the circus skills workshops.

10 With gloop from the clown's squirt gun.

ABOUT THE AUTHOR

Helen Chapman is an Australian author of eighty books who has been published in the United Kingdom, the U.S.A, New Zealand and Australia. She has travelled extensively and lived in America and England and is currently living in Australia.

For further information on Helen and her books visit: www.helenchapman.com

Helen has a special friend Rose Inserra who knows what her contribution has been to the ASH series and who can never be sufficiently thanked for it.